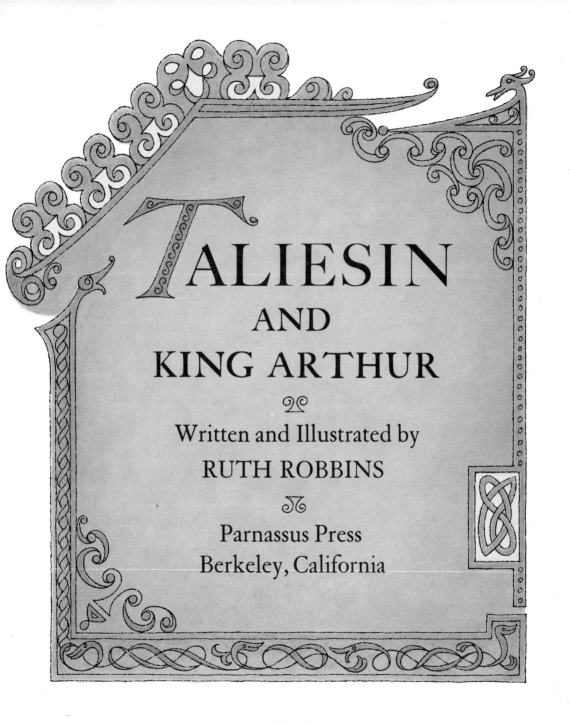

TALIESIN
AND
KING ARTHUR

Written and Illustrated by

RUTH ROBBINS

Parnassus Press
Berkeley, California

It was very long ago when the young poet Taliesin travelled from northern Wales to the court of King Arthur in Caerleon. This lad had the gift of telling a tale. His tales flowed like sparkling music while he plucked the strings of his harp.

As a child he had roamed the mountains and dark forests of his home: he had listened to the young streams and sat by the wild lakes hidden in high crags that slanted to the sea. The sea-blown winds had wrapped him in their moaning voices. He understood the secret of a leaf, a flower, a skylark in its truthful beauty. And he possessed a rare wisdom for one so young; he could sing of the future as well as the past.

Growing to a youth, Taliesin heard travellers and countrymen tell of King Arthur and the Round Table. He listened with quiet yearning to each story, imagined the beautiful city Caerleon, and longed to sing for the King. So, in the season when tender mosses crept over the misty bogs, he took up the harp he loved, stuffed a bag with bread and cheese, kissed his family farewell, and set off for the King's city.

On the day he first knelt before King Arthur, to sing a strange tale while he strummed his gentle harp, Taliesin amazed the King. "Your haunting story lingers upon the ear, it stirs the soul. Tell me, who are you?" spoke King Arthur.

"I am Taliesin, from the north country, your Majesty. One might call me a shepherd or a fisher; but my heart is filled with song and I would sing."

"Well then, poet Taliesin, for that is what you are, welcome to these halls. Stay a while in Caerleon and sing to us. It is like new rain falling, to hear your young voice."

So time after time the boy entertained King Arthur sitting with his knights of chivalry and the ladies of the castle. Each song astonished his listeners, as he told of men's deeds to come or of rites long buried with old bones. And it became a favored hour of the day when the King and his companions sat in wonder at the young bard's tales.

Now, in this bright December of the year, the stone walls and weathered gates of Caerleon began to warm with the festival of the Yule. Taliesin's eyes flashed joy at the sight of houses huddled close along furrowed lanes and white towers shining in the sunlight. With eager step he walked the cobbled streets to mingle in the celebrations of the season. He smelled the baker's cakes and heard the metal ringing on the forge. Through an arch and beyond the walls he followed the ritual of the Druids; the solemn procession into the forest, the cutting of the sacred mistletoe from the chosen oak.

His fair face tingled on frosty mornings in the old Roman amphitheatre where gallant knights displayed their skill in tilting, in tests of archery and throwing the lance. He saw horsemen with hounds and hawks ride into the surrounding woods. Riding with them were beautiful huntresses robed in scarlet.

These outdoor games brought good appetite to the noble people of the palace. They enjoyed in full spirit the feasting of the evenings in the great hall with Arthur and his Queen and his champions of the Round Table.

Taliesin, sitting at these merry banquets, had never known such a generous host as King Arthur. Roasted venison, salmon, and wild boar, steaming plum puddings and pancakes, spiced ale and ruby wine, were carried to the tables by elegant butlers and cup-bearers. Musicians played on flutes, pipes, and handbells: most notable was the King's chief harper whose brilliant talent was known in many courts. True was the proverb spoken in later years: *As merry as Christmas in Caerleon.*

To Arthur, a cherished custom of the Christmas festival was the Grand Meeting of the Bards. From far off heaths and hamlets of the island came poets, minstrels, ballad-makers, storytellers; each to sing his song; a contest of scholars and muses. And he who shone the brightest amongst his fellows would be honored by the King.

Arthur spoke to Taliesin of this special day, one he enjoyed above all the celebrations of the Yuletide. "It would please me much Taliesin, to hear you sing in this contest of poets. Young as you are, you will tell us a rare fine tale, I know."

The youth stood quiet, a blush of happiness crossed his brow. "Thank you my lord. If you think me worthy, I will sing."

Thus the bards of Britain gathered in the theatre on the day of Christmas Eve, and Taliesin's slim figure was a strange one in the group. Who is this Taliesin with the laughing face and mysterious eyes? they seemed to ask. They sat in a circle with Arthur their chief, and the Grand Esteddfod began.

Wondrous stories were told that day. Each bard had his turn. Aneurin the Famous sang of a battle; Prince Llywarch intoned on the brilliance of winter; Merlin, whom some called a magician, sang of his apple trees.

Last of all came Taliesin. As if to answer the questioning faces around him, he smiled and, bending to his harp, began his tale:

There once lived in Pemble Mere
a wise and serious wife named Ceridwen
who had good knowledge of magic lore
and enchantments.
She and her husband had been blessed
with a son and a daughter whom they held very dear.
So beautiful were the boy and girl
that when a third child, Avagddu, was born,
and he as foul and ugly as the other two were fair,
the mother brooded sorely over him.

She resolved to give him wisdom and understanding.
When he grows to a youth, she thought,
if men cannot admire him for his bearing,
they will respect him for his wit
and knowledge of all things.

So Ceridwen summoned up what she had learned,
and studied even more of magic mysteries.
Then she took a deep cauldron
and prepared to boil a brew of inspiration
for her son. Into the cauldron she placed
wild herbs, flowers, and plants of virtue.
Ceridwen searched the lonely moors and the
shadowy woods,
casting a spell on plant and flower.
The yarrow, the hyssop, the sweet eglantine;
heather-bell and the fern Adiantum; each
she plucked with certain care
for her mysterious brew.

She knew that it must boil and boil
for a year and a day, until three precious drops
of essence remained.
These would give Avagddu the power of prophecy.

Ceridwen put the little shepherd Gwion
to watch and stir the cauldron while she searched,
and nine nymphs came from the wooded shore
to raise and feed the flame.

So the woman went about her gathering
with devotion, in all seasons and weathers,
in the dawn and in the twilight.

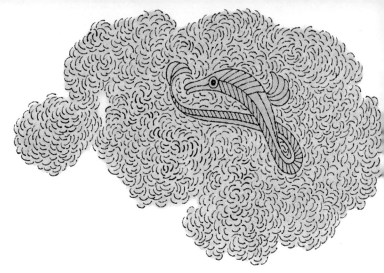

And when a year and a day had nearly
passed, little Gwion held the hideous child
as Ceridwen cast into the boil
one final, crowning sprig.

Up from the cauldron rose a great black smoke,
swelling and hissing; choking the
air with darkness.

When sunlight broke through the
veil of rising black,
little Gwion and the child were gone.
Ceridwen cried out. She found the fire dead,
the cauldron cold.

But deep in that cold vessel there lay
a sleeping child as fair as the morning star.
Ceridwen took him up; he woke and smiled.
She could see that it was not her own poor boy
nor little Gwion born again.
Why had all her labours come to ruin?
Her thoughts leaped wild and angry,
then she grew fearful of this new babe,
of the unknown power that might live in him.
Yet sweet he smiled and stretched his arms;
one could not destroy such beauty.
She wrapped him in a cloth of purple and gold
and placed him snug in a leather basket.
A mournful step she took;
she gave the basket to the sea and wind.

All the late day and into nightfall
the cradle swirled and glided with the wind.
It drifted on the spring tide
through a clear, still night.
Moonlight shone a flickering path upon the water,
and with the dawn the basket floated into
the weir of the fisher Elphin.

This Elphin was a poor, unlucky man
depending on his salmon catch from day to day.
He sometimes worked his fishery by moonlight,
anxious to know what the current had carried in.
The man's good wife came with him to the weir
and she kept vigil while her
husband looked to net the jumping fish.

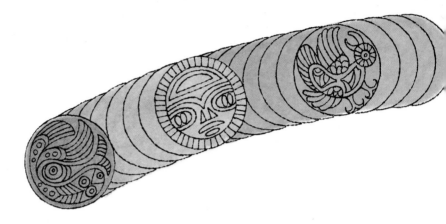

That daybreak Elphin found no salmon,
only the leather basket rocking on
shallow waves that lipped the water's edge.

He lifted the smiling, kicking baby
from its bed and Elphin's wife exclaimed
in wonder at its fair beauty.
"Behold — a radiant brow!
Taliesin, we shall name him."

And I am he: Elphin and his wife
took me as their own, and
we have enjoyed good fortune since that day.
I know well that Ceridwen's dreams were true,
her power protects me still.
I sing at will of images long gone;
the shadows of coming days tell me their secrets,
and this sweet harp whispers to me
the gift of poetry.

Taliesin lifted his head, his face aglow. "You who
have listened to my song now know the riddle of my
birth."

Not a flicker of sound broke the stillness of the
theatre. A moment later the spellbound audience burst
into cheers of joy and praise for Taliesin. King Arthur

stood and smiled splendidly at the young bard.

"Taliesin, your song has held us all enchanted; *you* have won the high honor of the day." And Arthur proclaimed Taliesin 'the greatest bard of them all.' And so he was known to be forever after.

That Christmas Eve the winter stars shone like a halo over the hills of Caerleon. Inside the torch-lit halls King Arthur and his people rejoiced in celebration.

Rejoice in Taliesin's Song.

Rejoice for the Glorious Coming Day.